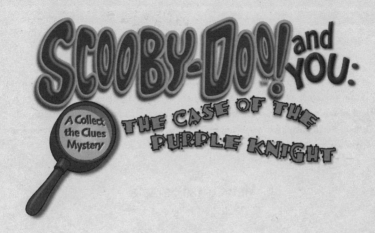

SCOOBY-DOO! and YOU: THE CASE OF THE PURPLE KNIGHT

A Collect the Clues Mystery

By James Gelsey

WORLDWIDE PUBLISHING™

SCHOLASTIC INC.

New York   Toronto   London   Auckland   Sydney
Mexico City   New Delhi   Hong Kong

ISBN 0-439-23155-8

12 11 10 9 8 7   3 4 5 6/0

Cover and interior illustrations by Duendes del Sur
Cover and interior design by Madalina Stefan

Printed in the U.S.A.

First Scholastic printing, February 2001

It's just about lunchtime, and you can hardly wait to meet the gang at Billy's Barn. You walk through the swinging red doors and find yourself inside a genuine barn. The horse stalls have been changed into private booths. The hayloft is set up for the band. And the henhouse out back has been turned into the kitchen, complete with a big, brick barbecue. The sweet and tangy smell of Billy's barbecue sauce tickles your nose and makes you sneeze.

"*Resundheit!*" Scooby calls from one of

the booths. You walk on over and find Scooby seated next to Shaggy at the table. Fred, Velma, and Daphne sit across from them.

"Hey, it's great to see you!" Velma says with a smile. "We picked this place because we know it's one of your favorites."

"Like, it's one of our favorites, too," Shaggy says. "Right, Scoob?"

"Right!" says Scooby.

"Shaggy, any place that serves food is one of your favorites," Velma replies.

"And what's wrong with that?" Shaggy asks. "A guy's gotta eat, you know."

"Rand rogs, roo," Scooby adds.

Everyone laughs as the waiter walks over. He's dressed in denim overalls and a big straw hat. He smiles and places a platter of food on the table.

"Man, this is my lucky day," Shaggy says. "All-you-can-eat barbecued corn on the cob." The waiter also dumps a handful of corn holders onto the table. Scooby picks one up.

"Hey, look at that," Shaggy says as

Scooby waves it through the air. "It's a sword for a teeny, tiny knight."

"I'm surprised you're joking about knights," Daphne says. "It's only been a few days since our close call with you-know-who."

"Zoinks!" Shaggy exclaims. "Did you have to remind me, Daph? Now I've lost my appetite."

"I'll believe that when I see it," Daphne says with a smile.

"I guess we should explain," Fred says. "Our last mystery involved the Purple Knight."

"And it was really something," Velma adds.

"Would you like to hear more about it?" asks Daphne. "And maybe even try to solve it yourself?"

You nod your head with excitement.

"We thought so," Daphne says. "That's why we came prepared with this." She hands you a small notebook. "Here's the Clue Keeper from our last mystery. Don't worry, I took pretty good notes. Everything that happened is in there."

"Remember to keep your eyes open for ⟐ ⟐ ," Fred explains. "That means you've met one of the suspects."

"And the ⟜ means you found a clue," Velma continues. "At the end of each entry,

we'll ask you some questions to help you organize things."

"Write down your notes in your own Clue Keeper," Daphne says. "And by the end of lunch, I'll bet you'll have solved *The Case of the Purple Knight.*"

"Good luck!" says Fred.

Clue Keeper Entry 1

Fred steered the Mystery Machine through a big stone gate. We drove along a gravel driveway to a parking lot.

"Well, gang, here we are," Fred said as he turned off the van. "Everybody out."

We all jumped out of the van and saw an enormous castle standing before us. There was even a real drawbridge.

"Jinkies! What a beautiful castle," Velma gasped. "It looks like something out of a story book."

"Or the King Arthur legend," I added.

"But it sure doesn't look anything like a furniture store," Shaggy said.

Fred, Velma, and I looked at Shaggy.

"What are you talking about, Shaggy?" Fred asked.

"Like, I thought 'The Round Table' was a furniture store," Shaggy replied. "That *is* the name of this place, isn't it?"

"Yes. But why would we go to a furniture store for dinner?" I asked.

"Like, that's what I want to know," Shaggy said with a shrug.

"Ree, roo," Scooby agreed.

"Shaggy, that castle in front of us is not a furniture store," I explained. "It's a *restaurant* called The Round Table."

"But it's more than just a place to eat. It has a King Arthur theme," Fred continued. "There's going to be a medieval jousting competition. We watch it while we eat."

"You mean, like, knights fighting on horseback?" Shaggy asked.

"Exactly," I said.

"And lots of medieval food, too," Velma

added. "We'll eat the way knights and ladies ate in the time of King Arthur. But we'll never get to it unless we go inside."

We walked over the drawbridge and into the castle. A shiny suit of armor stood just outside the entrance.

"Welcome to The Round Table," a voice said.

"Zoinks!" Shaggy exclaimed. "That suit of armor just spoke!"

"Take it easy, Shaggy," I said. "The voice didn't come from that suit of armor."

"It came from me," a man said, jumping out from behind the suit of armor. He was wearing a long purple robe and a crown on his head. "I'm King Murray, and welcome to The Round Table! You're our one millionth customer, so tonight you will be my special guests!"

"Unless the Purple Knight shuts us down," another voice added. We all turned and saw a man dressed in a court jester's costume walking toward us. For a guy who was supposed to make people laugh he sure wore a sad expression. 👁 👁

"Marshall, we don't have to bother these nice young people with such nonsense," King Murray said.

"I don't call mysterious notes about the curse of the Purple Knight nonsense," Marshall replied.

"C-c-c-curse?" Shaggy stuttered.

"I told you not to buy that crown," Marshall continued. "But you had to spend all of our money to get it. And now we're getting these threatening notes about a curse. If anything happens to that crown, we'll have to close the restaurant. We'll be ruined!"

"Stop worrying," King Murray said.

"Don't tell me what to do," Marshall shot back. "I offered to buy your half of the

restaurant but you wouldn't sell it. If I was running this place on my own, this never would have happened. Now I'm stuck with you and your crazy ideas!" Marshall Maxwell turned and stomped off into the castle.

"Sorry about that, kids," King Murray said. "My brother's always thought he could run this place better without me. But forget about that."

King Murray turned and faced the entrance to the castle. He raised his arms and yelled, "Follow me, friends. It's time for the royal treatment!"

"It looks like there's some kind of mystery about to unfold at The Round Table. But you saw the 👀 on page 8, right? Now take out your Clue Keeper and a pen, and answer these questions about the suspect you just met."

1. What is the suspect's name?

2. What is he doing at The Round Table?

3. Why would he want to cause trouble at The Round Table?

"Once you've answered these questions, read on!"

Clue Keeper Entry 2

We followed King Murray into the castle. He led us through a long hallway lined with suits of armor. "King Murray, was the crown your brother spoke about the one you're wearing?" I asked.

He shook his head and led us to the far end of the hallway, away from the other armor. There we saw another suit of armor. The metal had a deep purple color. The suit stood with its arms outstretched. A velvet, purple pillow rested across the arms. And on the pillow sat a beautiful, jewel encrusted crown. "*That* is the crown he's talking about," King Murray said proudly.

"Jinkies!" Velma gasped. "That crown must be very valuable."

"And very cursed," someone else said.

"Bentley Byron, what are you doing here?" asked King Murray.

"When I heard that the crown of Arthur was here, I had to come and see for myself," Bentley replied. "You know something this valuable belongs in a museum. My museum."

"Do you mean Arthur — as in *King* Arthur?" Velma asked.

"Yes," Bentley answered, studying the crown closely.

"What's the curse about?" Fred asked.

"Legend has it that King Arthur expelled one of his knights from The Round Table for trying to steal this very crown," Bentley explained. "Arthur then had Merlin, his wizard, cast a spell to protect the crown. If anyone but the rightful owner should ever wear the crown, he will be cursed by the ghost of that knight."

"Was that knight, by any chance, called the Purple Knight?" I asked.

"Quite right, young lady," Bentley answered. "You know, Murray, this crown would be, if you'll pardon the expression, the crowning touch to my medieval exhibit."

15

"No way, Bentley," King Murray insisted. "The crown stays here."

"The crown does not belong in a restaurant!" Bentley protested.

"The crown stays here," King Murray repeated.

"All right, have it your way," Bentley said. "I just hope it doesn't take a visit from the Purple Knight to help you change your mind."

Bentley Byron turned and walked back down the hallway.

"Excuse me, King Murray," Shaggy said.

"Yes?"

"Does the royal treatment you promised us include, like, dinner?" asked Shaggy.

"Shaggy!" Velma scolded. "That's not polite."

"That's all right," King Murray smiled. "In fact, dinner is our next stop. You'll get to enjoy a royal feast in the king's special box. Follow me."

We followed King Murray through another doorway and down another hall lined with shields, tapestries, swords, and other medieval things. We followed King Murray up a flight of steps and through a red curtain.

"Wow!" Fred gasped. "How cool is this?"

We looked out over an enormous circular arena. Colored flags hung along the walls. The floor was covered with dirt. Knights on horseback were riding around, practicing for the upcoming jousting competition.

"Real knights must have been very strong to ride around in those heavy iron suits," I commented.

"Oh, yes, Daphne, they were," King Murray agreed. "But these knights here are wearing a special material my brother created for us. It looks like a real suit of armor, but it's much lighter and much more flexible. However, it still gets just as hot as inside real armor."

King Murray then stepped to the edge of his box and raised his arms. The knights slowly stopped riding and looked at him.

"And now, let the games —"

"— and the food —" Shaggy whispered to Scooby.

"— begin!" shouted King Murray.

"I'll bet you spotted the 👁 👁 on page 14. Open up your Clue Keeper and answer these questions about him."

1. What is the suspect's name?

2. What is he doing at The Round Table?

3. Why would he want to cause trouble at The Round Table?

"After you've jotted down your answers, turn the page and continue reading."

Clue Keeper Entry 3

"I hope you enjoy the show," King Murray said. "And, of course, your meal, too. I have to get ready for my part in the show. I'll see you kids later." King Murray walked down a staircase from the front of the royal box onto the stadium floor.

A knight rode into the middle of the arena and the first of the jousting matches began. Behind us, a waiter came through the curtain carrying a big tray of food. He tried to balance the tray on one hand and take the plates of food off with the other. He reached for a plate, and the big tray started tilting.

"Whoooaaaaaa!" he yelled as he quickly grabbed the tray with both hands to balance it out.

"Here, let us help," Fred said. He stood up and took plates off the big tray. He handed them to me and Velma and we put them down on the table.

"Thanks," the waiter said. He looked around and then leaned down. "You know, I'm not really a waiter," he whispered. "My name is Wesley Warren, and I own Ye Olden Tymes. It's a restaurant on the other side of town. I was wondering if I could ask you kids some questions."

"Scooby, could you get the basket of rolls from Fred?" Shaggy interrupted.

"Rou ret," Scooby answered. He stood up and reached over to Fred's side of the table. Wesley Warren looked up and saw Scooby. He screamed and dived under the table.

"Are you all right, sir?" Velma asked. "That's just our dog, Scooby-Doo."

"Oh, a dog?" the waiter said as he stood up. "Thank goodness. I thought it was a horse. I'm deathly afraid of horses."

"Why are you here pretending to be a waiter?" I asked.

"Murray Maxwell and his restaurant have been stealing customers from my restaurant for years," Wesley complained.

"Stealing?" I asked.

"Well, not really stealing," he admitted. "But I used to have a booming business. Then the Maxwell brothers opened this place and now most people come here instead of to my place."

"That's a shame," I sympathized.

Wesley nodded. "I snuck in today disguised as a waiter so I could try to get a look around and see what his secret to success is. And when I find that secret, I'm going to give him a taste of his own medicine."

"Fred, you don't think that Purple Knight's going to show up soon, do you?" interrupted Shaggy.

"Why?" Fred replied.

"Because Scooby and I have few more courses to finish," Shaggy answered. "And we'd hate to have to eat and run."

"Who's the Purple Knight?" asked Wesley. "Some gimmick that Murray dreamed up?"

"No, just some creepy ghost who's supposed to be guarding the crown of King Arthur," Shaggy answered between bites.

Wesley's eyes lit up when he heard Shaggy.

"Really?" asked Wesley. "Is the crown of Arthur here?"

"I think you'd better go, Mr. Warren,"

Fred interrupted. "King Murray will be coming back soon, and he wouldn't be too happy to see you here."

"That's all right," Wesley said. "I was just going. Going to find the crown of Arthur, that is. Thanks for your help, kids. Anytime you want a free meal, come on over to Ye Olden Tymes."

Wesley Warren dashed through the curtain in the blink of an eye.

"Where'd the waiter go?" asked Shaggy. "Does this mean we can't get seconds?"

Fred's Mystery-Solving Tips

"**W**ell, this suspect is certainly an interesting character, isn't he? Did you spot the 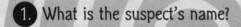 on page 21? Get out your Clue Keeper and answer these questions about him."

1. What is the suspect's name?

2. Why is he at The Round Table?

3. Why would he want to make trouble for The Round Table?

"Once you've finished, read on to see what happened next."

25

Clue Keeper Entry 4

As we finished eating, the second jousting contest started. We watched knights on horseback ride around the arena and joust at each other with long, sharp poles called lances.

Since we were sitting in the royal box, the knights would stop in front of us and bow before each match. After the third match, we heard a loud trumpet blast.

Everyone in the stadium quieted down as King Murray rode out into the middle of the arena on a white horse. He still wore his purple robe, but he wasn't wearing his crown. "Good evening, ladies and gentle-men!" he called. "This evening, I have some-thing very special to show you."

He clapped his hands, and a red curtain at the far end of the stadium parted. A knight carrying a lance in one hand slowly led a horse to the center of the stadium. The purple suit of armor from the hallway sat on the horse's back. The armor was still holding the crown of Arthur on the purple pillow.

"And now, ladies and gentlemen of the royal court, I present an item that has not been worn since the days of King Arthur," King Murray announced. "The crown of Arthur!"

King Murray reached over and carefully lifted the crown from the pillow. He held it with both hands and raised it over his head for all to see. Everyone started clapping. King Murray then slowly lowered the crown until it rested on his own head.

"Zoinks!" Shaggy suddenly exclaimed. "Like, I don't know about you, but I think I saw that purple suit of armor move!"

"That's probably just because the horse is moving," I noticed.

"No, Shaggy's right," Fred said. "Look!"

Sure enough, the purple suit of armor on the horse started moving.

It reached over and grabbed the lance from the knight who was holding the horse!

The knight dropped the reins and backed away. The purple suit of armor picked up the reins. It turned the horse to face King

Murray, who was now looking pretty scared himself.

"I am the Purple Knight!" a voice boomed from inside the suit of purple armor. "No one wears the crown of Arthur! Now you must pay!"

The Purple Knight gave the horse a light kick and started riding around the ring. King Murray sat on his horse in the middle, frozen with fear. The Purple Knight rode around the arena, faster and faster. He raised the lance and pointed it at King Murray. Then he gave the horse a swift kick and the horse started charging toward him.

"Like, I can't watch!" Shaggy shouted. He and Scooby covered their eyes.

King Murray closed his eyes, too.

The Purple Knight's lance speared the crown off King Murray's head!

Then the Purple Knight stopped his horse. "All of you must leave, or you, too, will be cursed by the Purple Knight!" he yelled.

Everyone in the stadium started clapping as the Purple Knight disappeared through the red curtain at the far end of the stadium. They thought it was all just part of the show. But I was pretty sure from the look on King Murray's terrified face that it wasn't.

"Man, I'll say one thing about that Purple Knight," Shaggy said. "He sure can ride a horse."

"Shaggy, I think you're on to something," I said. "Come on!"

We walked down the stairs to the stadium floor. Fred and Velma walked over to King Murray. Shaggy picked something up that had been left on the ground right by where the Purple Knight had been. It was a card or ticket.

"What does it say, Shaggy?" I asked.

"It's a ticket to a horse show from last week," Shaggy said, reading the ticket. "Like I said, that Purple Knight is into horses."

"Like, I guess I stumbled onto something. The only trouble is, I'm not sure what it is. Check out the ⚷ on page 31 and then answer these questions about it in your Clue Keeper. When you're done, maybe you can tell me what I discovered."

1. What is the clue?

2. What does this have to with the mystery?

3. Which of the suspects does this eliminate?

Clue Keeper Entry 5

King Murray, Fred, and Velma joined us. We showed them the ticket. "Let's go check out the stables," Fred suggested.

At that moment, Marshall Maxwell hurried over to us. The bells of his jester's cap jingled wildly. "Are you happy now, Murray!" he yelled, red-faced with anger. "Now see what you've done? That Purple Knight has our crown. We're ruined!"

"Leave me alone, Marshall," King Murray told him. "I have to help these kids solve this mystery."

King Murray brushed past his brother and led us through the red curtain. We found ourselves in the stable area. There was a row of horse stalls along each side of the stable. There was also lots of hay all over the floor.

"Rats!" I exclaimed.

"Rikes!" Scooby yelled. He jumped up into Shaggy's arms.

"What's the matter, pal?" Shaggy asked.

"Rats!" Scooby said.

"Scooby, I didn't mean I saw real rats," I explained. "I said it because I was hoping to follows the horse's hoofprints. With all this straw everywhere, we'll never figure out which way it went."

"Like, maybe the Purple Knight turned back into a ghost and disappeared so we'll never see him again and now we'll just have to go home and get something to eat," Shaggy said hopefully.

"Or maybe the Purple Knight left his horse right over there," I said. The horse the Purple Knight had been riding stood in the

34

last stall on the left. It was still panting from its big run.

"Did you find anything?" Fred asked as he and Velma walked over to join us.

"So far, just the horse," I said.

"King Murray went out to make sure no one leaves yet," Velma said.

"That should buy us some time," Fred added.

"How about buying us some water?" Shaggy asked. "Like, Scoob and I are thirsty from all this detective work."

"Reah, rhirsty," Scooby echoed. He picked up an empty water bottle from the floor and pretended to drink from it.

"Let me see that," I said. I examined the water bottle closely. "The bottle's still cold, which means that someone drank it recently."

"Someone who was very thirsty," Velma suggested.

"Someone who had just ridden a horse in a suit of armor," Fred exclaimed. "Someone like the Purple Knight!"

"I'll bet the Purple Knight must still be around here somewhere," I said.

"And the quickest way to find him is to split up and search," Fred suggested. "Velma and I will look around for more clues in here."

"Shaggy, Scooby, and I will go back to the hall of armor and see if we can find anything there," I said.

Daphne's Mystery-Solving Tips

"**W**ow, that's a pretty important clue you found on page 36. Take a few minutes to answer these questions in your Clue Keeper, and then read on to see how we tried to catch the Purple Knight."

1. What is the clue?

2. What does this clue tell you about the Purple Knight that chased Shaggy and Scooby?

3. Which of the suspects does this clue seem to fit?

Clue Keeper Entry 6

Shaggy, Scooby, and I walked around inside until we found the hall of armor. At the far end, we noticed that the purple suit of armor was missing.

"Hey!" I cried as a man scrambled along the wall toward the door. It was Wesley Warren. "What are you doing in here?"

"Oh, it's just you," he said. "I was afraid it was one of the Maxwell brothers. I don't want them to find me in here spying on their place."

"Like, do you know what happened to the

Purple Knight that was standing over there?" Shaggy asked.

"No. I took a wrong turn and ended up in their kitchen. While I was in there I decided to check out their menu. I just came into this room this very second," he replied.

I wondered if he was telling the truth. Had he dressed as the knight, then stashed the crown somewhere else? He certainly didn't have it now. "The crown's been stolen," I told him. "Please don't leave until we find out who did it."

"Oh, that's awful," he said. "Let me find Murray and see if I can help." He hurried out of the room.

I looked at Scooby and Shaggy. "I'm going to see what I can find in the next room. You two look around here. And stay out of trouble."

"Trouble? Us?" Shaggy asked. "Believe me, Daphne, trouble is the last thing Scooby and I want to find. The exit is the first thing, and trouble is the last. Well, maybe the snack bar is the first thing . . ."

"Oh, brother," I said as I left.

While I was gone — Shaggy told me later — he noticed a large tapestry hanging on the wall. It was a banquet of the all the knights of the Round Table. "You know, Scoob, it must've been pretty groovy to be a knight," Shaggy said. "I'll bet you got free food all the time."

"*Reaking rof rood,*" Scooby began.

"I'm with you, Scooby-Doo," Shaggy said. "I'll bet the restaurant's kitchen is down one of these halls."

Shaggy and Scooby left the hall of armor and started walking around. They soon came to the end of a hall. There were two doors in front of them.

"Okay, Scoob, do you want door number one or door number two?" Shaggy asked, pretending to be a game show host.

"*Rumber roo,*" Scooby answered.

"Number two it is," Shaggy said. "Let's see what you've won." Shaggy reached over and opened the door on the right.

"Zoinks!" Shaggy exclaimed. "It's the

Purple Knight!" Inside the opened door stood the purple suit of armor. Shaggy slammed the door shut.

"How about door number one?" Shaggy asked. He opened the other door.

"Rikes!" Scooby cried. *"Ruh Rurple Right!"* He jumped up into Shaggy's arms. The Purple Knight growled and reached out to grab them.

"Thanks for playing!" Shaggy said, slamming the door. "Now let's get out of here!" They turned and started running as the door opened. The Purple Knight chased Shaggy and Scooby down the hall and back into the hall of armor.

Shaggy and Scooby weaved between the suits of armor. They ran all the way to the end and ducked behind the last one. They sat perfectly still.

"I guess we lost him," Shaggy whispered.

"Wrong!" the Purple Knight roared from behind them.

"Rikes!" Scooby yelled, jumping into the air. He knocked into a suit of armor. It toppled sideways and started a chain reaction. The suits of armor fell over like a row of dominoes.

The sound was deafening! Shaggy and Scooby covered their ears.

When they turned around again, the Purple Knight was gone.

I ran down back to the hall of armor as soon as I heard the crashes. When I arrived, Fred and Velma were already there. Murray and Marshall Maxwell ran into the room from the opposite direction.

"My goodness!" King Murray cried. "What happened in here?"

"Shaggy, Scooby, are you all right?" Velma asked.

"It was the Purple Knight!" Shaggy exclaimed. "Both of them!"

"What do you mean 'both of them'?" I asked.

"Come on, we'll show you," Shaggy said.

Shaggy led us to the two doors. The first

purple suit of armor was still standing inside the door on the right.

"But if the armor is still here, then who chased your friends?" King Murray asked.

"The Purple Knight chased them, Murray!" Marshall exploded angrily. "You just don't want to face it, do you?" He stormed out of the room.

"Maybe it really is a ghost," King Murray said.

"I don't think so," Velma disagreed. "But who is doing this?"

"I have a hunch," I said. "But we'll have to prove it."

"Daphne's right," Fred agreed. "It's time to set a trap."

Velma's Mystery-Solving Tips

"I know you saw the  on page 46. It may not seem like much, but every clue helps get closer to solving the mystery. So take out your Clue Keeper and answer these questions about the clue."

1. What is the clue?

2. What does it have to do with the mystery?

3. What does this clue tell you?

"Once you're done, continue reading to see what else we found."

Clue Keeper Entry 7

"This isn't going to be easy," Fred said. "But I think there's a way we can get the Purple Knight to come out. We'll need to act fast. Daphne, Velma, and I will be waiting inside the arena. King Murray, we'll need to use some of the large horse blankets."

"No problem, Fred," King Murray replied.

"Great," Fred said. "Shaggy, you and Scooby will hang around here. When the Purple Knight shows up, let him chase you back to the arena. But make sure you go back through the stables."

"Like, why us?" Shaggy moaned.

"Because he knows you've seen the real purple armor," I explained. "He'll want to make sure you don't have a chance to tell anyone else."

"I got it, Daphne," Shaggy said. "But I think there's one problem."

"What's that?" I asked.

"Someone needs to convince Scooby to get it," Shaggy replied.

"Hey, Scooby," Velma said. "We need some help from the bravest dog we know. How about it?"

Scooby turned away from me and pretended not to hear.

"Will you help us for a Scooby Snack?" I asked. At the mention of the words, I could see Scooby's ears twitch with excitement. But Scooby still didn't say anything.

"How about two Scooby Snacks?" I offered.

Scooby jumped up. *"Rokay!"* he agreed. Velma and I each tossed a Scooby Snack into the air. Scooby gobbled them down.

"Then we'll see you in the arena," Fred said. "Just get him to chase you in, and we'll take care of everything else." Fred, Velma,

King Murray, and I walked back to the stadium to get ready.

Shaggy and Scooby stood by the doors for a few moments. At first, nothing happened. Then — Shaggy told me later — he heard a clanking sound. A sound like someone in heavy armor approaching.

"Scoob?" Shaggy asked.

"Reah?" Scooby said.

"Like, do you know the way back to the arena through the stables?"

Scooby thought for a moment.

"Ruh uh," he replied. *"Roo rou?"*

"Nope. I guess there's only one thing to do," Shaggy said, looking back down the hallway. "Run!"

The Purple Knight came running down the hallway at Shaggy and Scooby. They opened the left door and saw that it opened onto another hallway. They ran down that hallway, then another, and another.

"Up there, Scooby, quick!" Shaggy yelled. They ran through a heavy black curtain and found themselves inside the arena.

"Shaggy, Scooby, this way!" Fred called. He, Velma, and I were in the stands just over the entrance to the stables. We were ready to throw the horse blankets on the Purple Knight.

Shaggy and Scooby ran through the red curtain and into the stables. The Purple Knight ran out into the arena. He must have seen us duck down to hide, because he ran back through the black curtain.

Now the arena was empty again. A moment later, we heard Shaggy and Scooby shout. "Maaaaake waaaaaayyyyyy!" Shaggy yelled.

Suddenly, Scooby burst through the red curtain on horseback, trying very hard not to fall. The Purple Knight followed close behind, also on a horse. But where was Shaggy?

"Quick, grab a blanket!" Fred shouted.

We threw the blanket as the Purple Knight rode by, chasing Scooby.

But, at that moment, Shaggy ran out through the red curtain. The Purple Knight rode right past the blanket and it fell on Shaggy instead. Trapped beneath the heavy blankets, Shaggy fell to the ground.

"Here, Scooby!" King Murray shouted.

"Take this!" He held out a lance for Scooby to grab as he rode by.

Scooby reached out but missed it. The Purple Knight however grabbed it with ease. Scooby's horse ran by the pile of blankets just as Shaggy stood up.

The horse was frightened by Shaggy and kicked up its hind legs. Scooby went flying through the air!

Plop! He landed on the Purple Knight's horse!

"Relp! Raggy!" Scooby cried.

Scooby hugged the Purple Knight so tightly the knight couldn't see where he was going. The horse rode faster.

Suddenly, the tip of the Purple Knight's lance hit the ground. It got stuck in the dirt, flinging Scooby and the Purple Knight into the air.

Scooby landed on the pile of horse blankets just as Shaggy jumped out of the way. The Purple Knight flew through the red curtains.

We raced into the stable. The Purple Knight had landed in an empty horse stall. Fred and King Murray grabbed the Purple Knight to keep him from running away.

"Now let's see who's really inside this armor," Fred said.

"**W**ow, that was some adventure, wasn't it?" Daphne asks. "I was out of breath just writing about it."

"I'll bet you'll be able to solve this mystery in a jiffy," Velma says. "All you have to do is look at your notes in your Clue Keeper."

"Compare your suspects with the clues you found," Fred suggests. "See if you can figure out which clues match up with which suspects. When you identify the suspect who could be connected with all clues, you've solved your mystery."

"So take your time," Velma says.

Once you've figured out the mystery, turn the page and see what really happened.

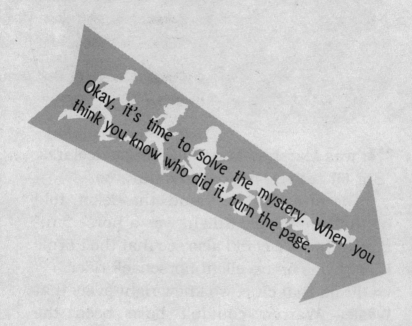

Okay, it's time to solve the mystery. When you think you know who did it, turn the page.

"It was Marshall Maxwell!" Velma declares. "But I'll bet you figured that out, too."

"The first clue we found, the ticket, told us that the Purple Knight was a horse fan," Fred says. "We could also see that the Purple Knight was an excellent horseback rider."

"From that clue, we knew right away that Wesley Warren couldn't have been the Purple Knight," Velma says. "He told us that he was deathly afraid of horses. Even Scooby-Doo scared him, remember?"

"So that left either Marshall or Bentley, or

a real ghost," Velma continues. "But once we found the next clue, the water bottle, we knew that there was definitely a real, live person involved."

"Make that a real, live thirsty person," Shaggy interjects.

"When Shaggy and Scooby found the real purple suit of armor in that closet, that's when we knew it had to be Marshall," Velma says. "Finding the real armor confirmed that the Purple Knight was only wearing a costume that looked like armor. And King

Murray told us that Marshall created a special material just for the knights to wear at the restaurant."

"So he made a costume that looked just like the real armor," Fred says. "He stole the crown so he could sell it and get their money back. He wasn't going to tell Murray about it, though. He'd wait until the restaurant went broke, then he'd buy out Murray's half so he could run it himself."

"But now, like, Murray has a new partner," Shaggy adds. "Wesley Warren and King Murray are combining their businesses."

"Well, I hope you're proud of yourself for solving this mystery," Velma says.

"King Murray was so proud that he gave Scooby a special honor," Velma says.

"That's right," Fred agrees. "He

made Scooby an official knight of King Murray's Round Table."

"Like, that's *Sir* Scooby to you," Shaggy says.

"Rooby-rooby-roo!" shouts Scooby.